ORANGE YOU GLAD YOU'RE NOT ME?

WHY HIM, AND NOT ME?! THIS SHOULD BE MY GRAPHIC NOVEL!

Annoying Orange is created by DANE BOEDIGHEIMER

SCOTT SHAW! – Writer & Artist

MIKE KAZALEH – Writer & Artist

LAURIE E. SMITH – Colorist

PAPERCUTZ™

NEW YORK

2 "Orange You Glad You're Not Me?"
"There's No Business as Annoying as Show Business!"
"Part of This Ridiculous Breakfast!"
"What's the Skinny on Mr. Fat-Citrus?"
"A Date is Not Just a Dried Fruit!"
"The Quest for the Golden Grail!"
"Not Everything He's Cracked Up to Be!"
Scott Shaw! – Writer & Artist
Laurie E. Smith – Colorist
Tom Orzechowski – Letterer
"Orange You Glad You're Not Me?"
Mike Kazaleh – Writer & Artist
Laurie E. Smith – Colorist
Tom Orzechowski – Letterer

Special thanks to: Gary Binkow, Tim Blankley, Dane Boedigheimer, Kristy Fagan,
Spencer Grove, Teresa Harris, Reza Izad, Debra Joester, Polina Rey, Tom Sheppard
Design & Production: Nelson Design Group, LLC
Director of Marketing: Jesse Post
Production Coordinator: Beth Scorzato
Associate Editor: Michael Petranek
Jim Salicrup
Editor-in-Chief

ISBN: 978-1-59707-390-5 paperback edition
ISBN: 978-1-59707-391-2 hardcover edition

Printed in Canada
May 2013 by Friesens Printing
1 Printers Way
Altona, MB ROG OBO

Distributed by Macmillan
First Printing

MEET THE FRUIT...

HERE'S A GUY WITH A LOT OF *APPEAL*...

YEAH! *ORANGE PEEL!* HA! HA! HA!

ORANGE

Since the debut of ANNOYING ORANGE #1 "Secret Agent Orange," the Orange-loving public has wondered on Internet Bulletin Boards and on school bathroom walls exactly how the world-famous fruity cast of the hit Cartoon Network TV series has been turned into graphic novel characters. Well, it turns out it wasn't all that difficult! Today's award-winning graphic novels tend to feature characters who have lead extraordinary lives. Harvey and Eisner Award Committees please take note—here at last is the powerful tale of a young orange who has dared to be... annoying!

PEAR

In keeping with a literary tradition that has included Steinbeck's Lenny and George and Marshall's Lenny and Squiggy, Pear is the character that Orange considers his best friend. That is if he were to consider such things. Pear spent considerable time posing for graphic novel artists Scott Shaw! and Mike Kazaleh in order to achieve a perfect likeness, and upon seeing the artistic results, Pear opined "whatever."

MIDGET APPLE

More concerned with self-image is Midget Apple. The graphic novel creators have found this particular prickly fruit to be the most difficult to please. "He keeps insisting that we draw him even bigger than Grapefruit!" a frustrated Scott Shaw! commented in an online interview with THE BEET's Heidi Macintosh. "But in the interests of journalistic truth—and because our editor told us to ignore Midget Apple—we're drawing him just as we see him. Small. Very Small."

PASSION FRUIT

I'M SIMPLY BESIDE MYSELF!

Such a potentially award-winning graphic novel saga must also focus on the characters who populate our hero's world—in this case the produce section of Daneboe's Supermarket. Making the transition from the computer screen to the TV screen and now onto the printed page (and then back on the computer screen in the digital edition!) Passion Fruit is once again cast in the role of the loyal, supportive female who clearly has affection for Orange despite his tendency to be… annoying. Yes, the women do like their bad boys!

MARSHMALLOW

I LOVE BEING ME!

ME TOO! YAY!

Perhaps there's no character in this amazing saga more mystifying than Marshmallow. Marshmallow is virtually the living embodiment of pure positivity despite being so out of place! Critics love such enigmatic characters and we love Marshmallow! Yay!

GRANDPA LEMON

Just as "Maus," the famed graphic novel by Pulitzer Prize-winning cartoonist Art Spiegelman, featured a dialogue between father and son, Grandpa Lemon is the voice of an earlier generation. In the already classic "The Salad Days of Grandpa Lemon," from ANNOYING ORANGE #1 "Secret Agent Orange," not only was the story particularly poignant, Grandpa Lemon made the brave choice to play his role wearing his never-before-seen glasses. A controversial decision that got him in hot water with the TV show's producers. But lemons are used to being in hot water, so it was no big deal.

GRAPEFRUIT

Grapefruit, convinced he's being held back by the limitations of the small screen, is convinced that he may actually thrive in the graphic novel format. Comparing himself to such classic comics characters as "The Incredible Hulk" and "Stumbo," Grapefruit believes comics may be an ideal showcase for his massive muscular macho persona. At press time, it seems the jury is still out on that one, but who knows?

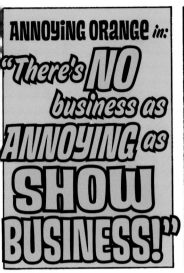

ANNOYING ORANGE *in:*

"There's **NO** business as **ANNOYING** as **SHOW BUSINESS!**"

WHAT'S WRONG, ORANGE? YOU AND YOUR FRUITY FRIENDS SEEM KINDA *DEPRESSED!*

OH, WE'RE JUST *BUMMED-OUT* THAT WE HAVEN'T HAD MUCH LUCK WITH ACHIEVING OUR *DREAM-JOB--*

--NAMELY, GETTING OUR-SELVES JOBS IN THE *ENTERTAINMENT INDUSTRY!*

"WE EVEN AUDITIONED FOR A BIG-SHOT HOLLYWOOD TALENT SCOUT! IT COST US AN *ARM* AND A *LEG,* TOO-- NOT THAT WE HAD A *SINGLE* ARM OR LEG AMONG US!"

"THE FIRST GIG HE SNAGGED FOR US WAS ON A FANCY-SCHMANCY *COOKING SHOW* ON TV..."

TODAY, I'M GOING TO DEMONSTRATE HOW TO PREPARE A DELICIOUS *SUMMER SALAD!*

IT'S LIGHT, IT'S REFRESHING, IT'S INEXPENSIVE, AND *BEST* OF ALL, IT'S *LOW* IN CALORIES!

HOWZAT? FUNNY STUFF, HUH?

≥GROAN!≤

≥SIGH!≤

≥YECCH!≤

≥FEH!≤

UH-OH!

YAHHH! HELP!

WE'RE NOT ROTTEN--

--WE JUST ACT THAT WAY!

YOWL

BOO! BOO!

YOU STINK!

WE WANT OUR MONEY BACK!

OMIGOSH! WERE YOU GUYS HURT?

NAH, WE JUST GOT A FEW BRUISES AND I SCRAPED MY RIND!

"THEN, WE GOT BOOKED ON A TV GAME SHOW! AT FIRST, IT SEEMED LIKE IT'D BE EASY, BUT THEN..."

the BIG PAYOFF!

WELCOME TO BIG BUCK$, THE GAME SHOW WHERE EVEN AN IDIOT CAN BECOME A ZILLIONAIRE-- JUST BY PULLING A LEVER!

RIGHT, CHUCK!

OOH! AHH! WOW!

AND THIS IDIOT JUST CAN'T WAIT TO PLAY! ≥UMPH!≤

YANK

"AND THAT'S WHEN IT ALL WENT BAD... REAL BAD!"

AHHH! WHOAAA! ≥BLECHHH!≤

TWIRL

SO YOU GOT *FIRED*?

YEAH-- AFTER WE ALL *THREW UP* ON THE SHOW'S *PRODUCER*!

HEY, I'VE GOT A FRIEND WHO'S THE PRODUCER OF A SPECTACULAR *DANCE REVIEW*! HERE'S HER PHONE NUMBER!

555-1951

A FEW DAYS LATER...

Ring Ring

Dansboe's

HELLO, NERVILLE SPEAKING! OH, HI, ORANGE! HOW DID THINGS WORK OUT WITH MY FRIEND, THE DANCE PRODUCER?

AND I *DO* MEAN *"THE TOP"*!

KEEP *DANCIN'*, CARMEN! WE'RE *IN THE GROOVE* NOW!

CLAP CLAP

CLAP

THINGS COULDN'T BE BETTER! WE FINALLY MADE IT TO THE *TOP* OF *SHOW BUSINESS*!

THE END!

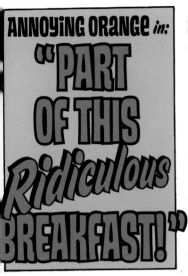

ANNOYING ORANGE in:

"PART OF THIS Ridiculous BREAKFAST!"

WOW, I ACTUALLY GOT SOME *MAIL!* MAYBE IT'S FROM A BEAUTIFUL *FAN-FRUIT!*

HMMM, IT'S FROM A BIG-TIME *CEREAL MANUFACTURER!*

"DEAR MR. ORANGE..."

WHAT'S *UP,* ORANGE?

THIS IS WHAT'S UP-- SO *READ IT!* I'LL EVEN HELP YOU WITH THE *BIG WORDS!*

"DEAR MR. ORANGE, I REPRESENT THE MILLSTONE CEREAL CO. WE WANT YOU AND YOUR FRIENDS TO APPEAR ON OUR *FRUITY POLYHEDRONS* CEREAL BOXES AND TV COMMERCIALS."

"WE LOOK FORWARD TO A LONG AND EXTREMELY PROFITABLE RELATIONSHIP." WOW, THESE GUYS ARE *SERIOUS,* ORANGE!

I ESPECIALLY DIG THAT *"EXTREMELY PROFITABLE"* PART! SO, *WHAT* IS A *"POLYHEDRON,"* ANYWAY?

SOON, NERVILLE AND HIS FRUITY FRIENDS GO ONLINE TO LEARN MORE ABOUT THE CEREAL COMPANY...

HERE IT IS, GANG-- A TV COMMERCIAL FOR MILLSTONE'S *FRUITY POLYHEDRONS* CEREAL!

WELL, WHY WASTE TIME? *CLICK ON* THAT BAD BOY!

CLICK

NO, THAT WAS *TIPPI HEDREN!* A POLYHDREN IS "A GEOMETRIC SOLID IN THREE DIMENSIONS WITH FLAT FACES AND STRAIGHT EDGES."

NAHHH! WHAT IS IT *REALLY?* HAHAHAHAHA-HAAA!

OKAY, YOU LITTLE RASCAL, THAT FRUIT TRUCK IS ONE OF THE MOST *IMPORTANT* FACTORS IN THE MANUFACTURING OF *FRUITY POLYHEDRONS...*

THAT REMINDS ME! I REALLY WANT TO MEET THE *FRUIT* YOU USE TO MAKE THAT CEREAL!

WELL, THAT'S *IT!*

THAT'S THE FRUIT THAT'S PART OF OUR WHOLE *PROCESS!* IT LOOKS DELICIOUS, DOESN'T IT?

SO, CAN I MEET YOUR FRUIT?

THAT'S *IMPOSSIBLE.* Y'SEE, THAT FRUIT TRUCK NEVER ACTUALLY STOPS HERE!

WHAT? HOW CAN YOU MAKE FRUITY-GEOMETRIC-SOLIDS-IN-THREE-DIMENSIONS-WITH-FLAT-FACES-AND-STRAIGHT-EDGES WITHOUT ANY *FRUIT?!*

YEAH! I'M PERPLEXED! OUTRAGED, TOO!

OBVIOUSLY, YOU'RE BOTH *NEW* TO THE KIDDIE CEREAL BIZ! WE ADHERE TO THE RIGOROUS STANDARDS SET FOR THE FOOD INDUSTRY!

FRUITY POLYHEDRONS QUALIFIES TO USE "FRUITY" IN THEIR NAME ONLY BECAUSE THAT FRUIT TRUCK DRIVES PAST OUR FACTORY AT LEAST *TWO TIMES* A DAY!

SO, I SIGNED THE DEAL WITH A CLEAR CONSCIENCE-- KNOWING NO FRUIT WILL EVER BE HARMED FOR THIS CEREAL! HAHAHAHA-HAHAAA!

END

GRAPEFRUIT in: "What's the SKINNY on FAT MR. SOUR-CITRUS?"

GRAPEFRUIT, WHAT ARE YOU *DOING?*

I'M *WEIGHING* MYSELF.

BUT, *WHY?*

BECAUSE I'M GETTING *FAT*, THAT'S WHY!

BUT GRAPEFRUIT ARE SUPPOSED TO BE *BIG* AND *ROUND* AND *HEAVY!* BESIDES, GRAPEFRUIT IS KNOWN TO BE ONE OF THE VERY *HEALTHIEST FRUITS* OUT THERE!

REALLY?

THEN HOW COME ALL THE OTHER FRUIT ARE ALWAYS TEASING ME ABOUT BEING FAT?!

LATER THAT DAY, AT THE PUBLIC LIBRARY...

HEALTH AND NUTRITION

HEALTH AND NUTRITION

HEALTH AND NUTRITION

HEALTH AND NUTRITION

HEALTH AND NUTRITION

QUIET- *THIS* MEANS YOU, ANNOYING ORANGE!

HMMM... DIET BOOKS... DIET BOOKS... DIET BOOKS... DIET BOOKS...

A-HA! DIET BOOKS! LET'S SEE WHAT THEY'VE GOT...

16

ONLY CHECKING OUT *ONE* BOOK TODAY, SIR?

YEAH, BUT IT'S THE *RIGHT* BOOK-- FOR *ME!* AND WHEN I RETURN IT, YOU WON'T EVEN RECOGNIZE ME!

DAYS PASS...

HEY, GANG! HAS ANYONE SEEN GRAPEFRUIT LATELY?

TRUST ME, NERVILLE, IF GRAPEFRUIT WERE HERE, YOU COULDN'T *HELP* BUT SEE HIM! *HAHAHAHAHAHAHA!*

OH, ORANGE, BE *NICE!*

YEAH, ORANGE! I'M KINDA *WORRIED* ABOUT THE BIG LUG!

WELL, I GET KINDA WORRIED ABOUT THE *LUG NUTS* ON THE FRUIT CART'S WHEELS! *HAHAHA-HAHAHA!*

IT'S *THAT* SORT OF TEASING THAT PROBABLY MAKES GRAPEFRUIT WANT TO AVOID US!

YES, HE LIKES TO ACT LIKE A TOUGH GUY, BUT *DEEP INSIDE,* I THINK THAT GRAPE- FRUIT IS MORE SWEET, SOFT AND SENSITIVE, THAN ANY OF US REALIZE!

IN FACT, I WOULDN'T BE SURPRISED IF HE--

SHRIEK!

WHAT?! THIS BOOK SAYS TO LOSE WEIGHT, JUST EAT NOTHING BUT *GRAPEFRUIT--* AND SO I *DID!*

BUT APPARENTLY I'M *NOT* THE ONLY ONE!

THE GRAPEFRUIT DIET

END

19

"ORANGE you GLAD you're not ME?"

MIKE KAZALEH, Story & Art
LAURIE E. SMITH, Color
TOM ORZECHOWSKI, Letters
JIM SALICRUP, Edits

HI, ORANGE! I'VE JUST FINISHED MY LATEST AND GREATEST INVENTION! WHAT DO YOU THINK OF IT? *TERRIFIC*, EH?

IT LOOKS NIFTY, NERVILLE! BUT SOMEBODY ALREADY INVENTED THE GAS CHAMBER!

IT'S NOT A GAS CHAMBER! IT'S A *TIME MACHINE!* IT HAS BEEN MY LIFELONG AMBITION TO WITNESS THE FIRST MAN IN HISTORY EAT A RAW OYSTER, AND THIS MAGNIFICENT MACHINE WILL MAKE IT POSSIBLE!

A TIME MACHINE, HUH? UNLESS YOU'VE BEEN KEEPING UP WITH YOUR YOGA LESSONS, I DON'T THINK YOU'LL BE ABLE TO FIT INSIDE OF IT.

23

LOOKS LIKE A PRETTY GOOD GUILLOTINE TO ME. A REAL *CUT ABOVE!* WHAT'S THE PROBLEM, FRENCH ONION?

THE PROBLEM, MY SEEDY FRIEND, IS THAT MARIE IS A *LETTUCE*...

...AND HOW THE HECK CAN YOU BEHEAD SOMEBODY WHO IS *ALL HEAD?* STILL, WE MUST KEEP TRYING SO THAT WE MAY RID OUR COUNTRY OF THIS ENEMY OF THE PEOPLE!

WELL, I GUESS OL' MARIE SHOULD'VE QUIT WHILE SHE WAS AHEAD! GET IT? *A-HEAD!* GET IT? HAHAHAHAHA!

HEY! WHAT'RE YOU GUYS SO *SORE* ABOUT? I THOUGHT SHE WAS AN ENEMY OF THE PEOPLE!

YES! AN ENEMY OF THE *FRENCH* PEOPLE! WE CAN'T ALLOW SOME FOREIG FRUIT TO MAKE FUN OF *OUR QUEEN!*

YEESH! THESE GUYS ARE A ROYAL PAIN!

hmmmmm PING

Swish
CHUNK
CHUNK
CHUNK

hmmmmm

PING

ALRIGHT, ANGRY ORANGE! COME OUT WITH YOUR HANDS U--

--WELL, ANYWAYS, COME OUT! I'VE GOT YOU **SURROUNDED!**

JUST A MOMENT! JUST A **MOMENT!** I'VE GOT SOME GOULASH ON THE STOVE...

OH! IT'S YOU. WELL, WHAT DO YOU **WANT?**

I'M HERE TO STOP YOU FROM TRYING TO HARM NERVILLE...! SO **STOP** TRYING TO HARM NERVILLE!

HA! YOU'RE TOO LATE! I'VE **ALREADY** MET UP WITH A PAST VERSION OF MYSELF, AND HE'S ALREADY ON HIS WAY TO YOUR PAST! A **WEEK** PAST, TO BE EXACT!

AND WHAT HE, OR RATHER **I**, HAVE IN STORE FOR NERVILLE, YOU DON'T WANT TO KNOW! **HA HA HA HA HA!**

SO... SHALL I SET OUT ANOTHER PLACE SETTING FOR SUPPER?

41

43

I CAN HARDLY BELIEVE THAT ACTUALLY *WORKED.*

STILL, SOMETHING'S WRONG. *I'M* STILL HERE, EVEN THOUGH I'M IN THE WRONG TIME TOO. SHOULDN'T I HAVE GONE BACK TO--

PING

--MY *OWN* TIME?

WHOA! THAT WAS A MAJORLY WEIRD TRIP! THE *NEXT* TIME I GO TRAVELLING THROUGH TIME AND SPACE, I'M GONNA TAKE A GPS SYSTEM WITH ME!

TOO BAD I HAD TO DESTROY THE TIME MACHINE. AT LEAST I WAS ABLE TO SAVE NERVILLE AND PREVENT THE DESTRUCTION OF HIS FINE BRAIN!

GIBBER GIBBER GIBBER GIBBER GIBBER GIBBER GIBBER GIBBER GIBBER GIBBER GIBBER

DANGER! *PANIC!* THREATS TO YOUR PERSONAL *SAFETY!*

CHIP

CHEAP

IT'S GOOD TO SEE NERVILLE BACK TO HIS OLD NUTTY SELF!

WHAT'RE YA *DOIN'* NERVILLE? BUILDING ANOTHER TIME MACHINE?

TIME MACHINE? WHAT ARE YOU TALKING ABOUT? I'M MAKING A MACHINE THAT WILL TWIST SUNBEAMS INTO THE SHAPE OF PRETZELS!

YOU BRING THE SALT AND MUSTARD!

A SUITABLE *TWIST ENDING* TO A TIME-TESTED, TONGUE-TWISTING TALE!

END.

46

THE TIME: 2:00 A.M... THE PLACE: NERVILLE'S APARTMENT...

BLEEP BLEEP BLEEP

WHUHHH? BUT I DON'T WANT TO GO TO SCHOOL TODAY, MOM...

ORANGE, IF THIS IS ANOTHER ONE OF YOUR STUPID KNOCK-KNOCK JOKES--

NERVILLE, THIS IS YER BOSS, MR. MANGEL-MANNER!

GRAB A MOP AND GET YOUR KEISTER DOWN TO DANEBOE'S SUPER-MARKET! THERE'S AN EMERGENCY!

WH-WH-- WHAT EMERGENCY?!

A HEAVY RAINSTORM HAS FLOODED THE STORE! OUR STOCK IS GETTIN' MORE WATERLOGGED BY THE MINUTE!

GOTCHA, BOSS! I'LL SEE WHAT I CAN DO!

YOU BETTER, OR THERE'S GONNA BE A ONE-MAN DOWN-SIZING, IF YA GET MY DRIFT!

I'M ALREADY SOAKED, SO HOW MUCH WETTER CAN IT POSSIBLY BE INSIDE?

CERRADO CLOSED

SPLOOSH

WELL, I GUESS THAT ANSWERS THAT!

I WISH I'D WORN MY HIGH-RISE JEANS...

OKAY, LET'S THROW A LITTLE LIGHT ON THE SUBJECT, SHALL WE?

CLICK

YUP, IT'S FLOODED, ALL RIGHT...

...REALLY DARK, TOO!

BUT I THINK I SEE SOMEONE OR SOMETHING MOVING AROUND IN HERE! HELLO? IDENTIFY YOURSELF, PLEASE! EXCUSE ME? HEY! HEY--

SPLISH SPLOSH SPLISH SPLOSH

HEY, APPLE! I'D LEND YOU A HAND-- BUT I DON'T *HAVE* ANY HANDS! HAHAHA-HAHAHAAA!

YANK

CONVERSION MODE: EPIC AQUATIC

TRANSFORM

SO HOW DO YOU LIKE *THEM* APPLES?

FRANKLY, I'D STILL PREFER A *DONUT*-- A *BAGEL*, EVEN! (HOLD THE CREAM CHEESE AND LOX, PLEASE.)

HOW DO YOU GUYS LIKE OUR NEW AWESOME *VESSEL?*

PSHAW! *"AWESOMELY EPIC"* IS MORE LIKE IT!

NOW, LET'S GO FIND NERVILLE AND BRING HIM SAFELY BACK!

RIGHT! BUT FIRST, WE NEED TO CHOOSE OUR SHIP'S CAPTAIN! ANY *NOMINATIONS?*

ME!

ME!

ME!

ME!

ME!

OH-KAYYY.

SINCE THIS PERSON WAS THE *ONLY* ONE OF US-- BESIDES ALWAYS-HUMBLE YOURS TRULY-- WHO *DIDN'T* NOMINATE HIMSELF OR HERSELF FOR THE JOB, I'D LIKE TO NOMINATE MARSHMALLOW AS THE CAPTAIN OF THE U.S.S. FRUIT CART!

WHADDAYA *THINK,* FOLKS?

YAY!

FULL SPEED AHEAD INTO THE MURKY HEART OF DARKNESS... 'CAUSE THAT'S WHAT WE *DOOOOO!*

49

SOON, MARSHMALLOW AND THE CREW APPROACH THE RARELY-VISITED EDGE OF THE PRODUCE DEPARTMENT...

WELL, SO FAR, SO GOOD...

HEY, PEAR! YOU REALLY PUT THE *"ODD"* IN *"ODYSSEY"*! HAHA-HAHAHAHAAA!

SUDDENLY...

HEY, GANG! CHECK OUT *THAT!*

DO MY INTENTIONALLY CREEPY-LOOKING *EYES* DECEIVE ME--

--OR IS THAT A GIANT POTATO WITH ONLY *ONE EYE?!* Y'KNOW, A *TATER-CLOPS!* OR A *CYCLATO!* OR A-- A *CYCLOPS POTATO!* OR SHOULD THAT BE A *"POTATO CYCLOPS"?*

RRRAWWW!

YEAH, WE *GET* IT-- YOU'RE *RAW,* YOU BIG *SPUD!*

HEY, *ONION!* HEY, *KNIFE!* A LITTLE *HELP* HERE, PLEASE?

YOU CALL, ORANGE?

ACTUALLY, IT WAS MORE LIKE A *CRY!* YOU DIG?

GOTCHA, ORANGE!

SLICE

SLICE

SLICE

THAT WAS QUICK THINKING, ORANGE!

YEAH, THE FUMES FROM ONION IS MAKING THE POTATO CYCLOPS *CRY!* IT CAN'T SEE A THING-- INCLUDING *US!*

WAHHH!

NEXT, THE U.S.S. FRUIT CART ENTERS THE PARTIALLY-SUBMERGED, MISTY REALM KNOWN IN DANEBOE'S SIMPLY AS THE "FROZEN FOODS DEPARTMENT"...

FROZEN WASTES, DEAD AHEAD!

LET'S HOPE THIS EPIC JOURNEY ISN'T A FROZEN WASTE OF OUR TIME!

HEY, LOOK! THOSE BIG COOLER DOORS ARE SWINGIN' OPEN!

MAYBE THEY'RE PREPARING TO GIVE US A WARM WELCOME?

BUT JUST LISTEN TO 'EM, PASSION FRUIT! DOES THAT SOUND WARM OR WELCOMING?

I'M A-GONNA DELIVER THE GOODS-- OF YOUR DESTRUCTION!

DOCTORS ARE RIGHT-- I'M NOT GOOD FOR YOUR HEALTH!

I PUT THE "HURT" IN FROZEN YOGHURT!

OH, THEIR ICY THREATS MAKE MY JUICE RUN COLD! CAPTAIN MARSHMALLOW, WHAT SHOULD WE DO?

DON'T WORRY!

LASSOS AT THE READY, CREW?

AYE, CAPTAIN MARSHMALLOW!

ROPE THOSE TUBES OF LINIMENT SALVE OFF THE SHELVES ON OUR STAR-BOARD SIDE!

AYE, CAPTAIN MARSH-MALLOW!

SALVES & OINTMENTS

GLOM
GLOM
GLOM
GLOM

NOW PULL 'EM ABOARD AND SQUEEZE OUT THE GOO INSIDE! AIM CAREFULLY, NOW!

AYE, CAPTAIN MARSH-MALLOW!

Squirt
Squirt
Squirt

HEAT
HEAT
INSTANT

SEE? THEY CALM RIGHT DOWN WHEN YOU COVER 'EM WITH HEAT-GENERATING PETROLEUM! YAY!

AIEEE! IT BURNS!

AYE, CAPTAIN MARSH-MALLOW!

I'M MELTING... MELTING!

OH, WHAT A WORLD, WHAT A WORLD...!

THAT WAS BRILLIANT, CAPTAIN MARSHMALLOW! YOU AREN'T NEARLY AS *SOFT* AND *SQUISHY* AS YOU LOOK!

YEAH, NOT HALF-BAD FOR A CONFECTION THAT CONSISTS OF SUGAR, CORN SYRUP, WATER, AND GELATIN THAT HAS BEEN SOFTENED AND WHIPPED TO A SPONGY CONSISTENCY, HUH?

THAT'S ESPECIALLY REASSURING, SINCE WE'RE ABOUT TO SAIL DOWN THE AISLE OF THE SUGAR-CRAZED *GRAIN TRUST!*

HOLY *CRAP!* THOSE GUYS ARE *INSANE!*

THEY SURE *ARE*-- AND BY THAT, I MEAN *"CRAP"!* HAHAHAHAHAHAAA!

MAYPOO BRAN · WHEAT SLEAZIES · NUTTY GRAPESHOT · APPLE JERKS

JUNK FOODIES · BRIX · OATMEALY WORMS · SNEERY-O'S · PHROOT BLOOPS

RICE KINKYS · ALPHA-BLITZ · CAVEMAN COCOA-CRUNCH · GOLDEN GRANOLA GLOBS · CHAFF FLAKES

ARNIE, MY *FRUITY FOSSILS!*

THEY'RRRE *ADEQUAAATE!*

FAITH AND BEGORRAH, THEY'RE AFTER ME *YUKKY SHAM-ROCKS!*

FRUITY FOSSILS · SUGAR FROSTED DANDER FLAKES · YUKKY SHAMROCKS

AS THE CAPTAIN, I NEED A PLAN! BUT I DON'T REALLY HAVE ONE!

AHRRR, ME LI'L *MARSH-MATEY!* WHY NOT *TRICK* 'EM INTO USIN' THEIR SUGAR-FUELED MADNESS AGAINST EACH OTHER?

SAILOR SPOON

THAT'S A *SWEET* SOLUTION! YAY!

AHRRR, I'D DO ANYTHING TO HELP A FELLOW *SEAMAN...*

...OR *SEAWOMAN...* OR WHATEVER IT IS YOU BE!

THAT WAS A *BRILLIANT IDEA,* CAPTAIN MARSH-MALLOW!!

AHOY, GRAIN TRUST! MY CREW AND I ARE CURIOUS-- WHICH ONE OF YOUR CEREALS CONTAINS THE *MOST SUGAR?*

FRUITY FOSSILS ARE THE SUGARIEST! AN' I'LL *GABBA-ZABBA CLUB-CLOBBER* ANY-ONE WHO SAYS OTHERWISE!

MY SUGAR FROSTED DANDER FLAKES ARE THE *GRRREATEST* SOURCE OF *SUGAR* KNOWN TO KIDS! THINK I'M WRONG? WELL, YOU WON'T BE THINKING AT ALL, AFTER I *BITE OFF* YOUR NOGGIN!

YER BOTH FULL OF BLARNEY! ME YUKKY SHAMROCKS CONTAIN MORE SUGAR THAN YER TWO CEREALS COMBINED! AN' I'LL USE MY *SHAMROCK SHILLELAGH* TO *WHACK* ANYONE WHO DISAGREES WITH ME!

OH, ANY SEA-FARER WORTH HIS OR HER *SALT* WOULD HAVE DONE IT! RIGHT, SAILOR SPOON?

AYE-AYE, MARSH-MATEY! AHRRR, SAFE SEAS TO YE!

FRUITY FOSSILS · SUGAR BOMBS · SUGAR FROSTED DANDER FLAKES · ALPHA-BLITZ · YUKKY SHAMROCKS · WHEAT SLEAZIES · BERRY EDIBLES

AS FOR YOUR HUMAN FRIEND, WE *HAVE* SEEN HIM--

--AS YOU CAN *SEE!* ⋚ARF ARF ARF!⋚

NERVILLE! YOU'RE *OKAY!*

ER, UH, Y'KNOW... "OKAY" FOR A PERSON WITHOUT A *RIND!*

WHAT HAPPENED, NERVILLE?

HOW DID YOU GET CAPTURED BY THE *TRIBE* OF THE *LOST?*

AND WHERE DID ALL OF THIS WATER COME FROM? DID YOU FORGET TO TURN THE *BATH FAUCET OFF?* HAHAHAHA-HAHAAA!

NO-- A *RAINSTORM* FLOODED DANEBOE'S AND MY BOSS CALLED ME TO COME IN AND CLEAN UP! BUT WHEN I DID, THESE DUDES TOOK ME AS THEIR *CAPTIVE!*

AND YOU'LL REMAIN OUR CAPTIVE UNTIL YOU PASS A *TEST*-- THE TEST OF YOUR *SHELF-LIFE!*

WE'LL RELEASE YOU, BUT ONLY IF YOU CAN LOCATE THE *GOLDEN GRAIL,* THE PORTAL TO THE *WORLD BELOW!* IT'S WHAT HAS CAUSED THE RISING OF THE WATER IN HERE!

AND IF YOU FAIL TO LOCATE IT, YOU WON'T BE ABLE TO HALT THE WATER'S *RISE*-- AND WE'LL BE FORCED TO OFFER YOU TO THE *GUARDIANS* OF THE *GOLDEN GRAIL!*

OUR HUMAN FRIEND IS ABOUT TO BE *SACRIFICED* TO A NON-EXISTENT DEITY! *YAY!*

SO NOW THAT THE BRASS FLOOR-DRAIN IS OPEN, THE FLOOD WATERS ARE BEGINNING TO RECEDE!

BUT WHAT DO I DO WITH THESE SOGGY OLD COUPONS?

UHH... REDEEM 'EM?

Gurgle

AND SPEAKING OF REDEMPTION, WE'RE ALLOWING ALL OF YOU TO LEAVE IN PEACE!

LIKE ME, YOU'RE DANGEROUS! UNLIKE ME, YOU'VE GOT A CODE OF HONOR! YAY!

WITHIN MINUTES, THE SUN RISES AND DANEBOE'S DAY BEGINS...

WELL, THAT'S THE LAST OF THE MOPPING...

Daneboe's

...ALL THAT'S LEFT FOR ME TO DO IS TO REPLACE THE STORE'S STOCK THAT SUSTAINED WATER-DAMAGE!

SO WATER YOU WAITIN' FOR, NERVILLE? GET CRACKIN', KID! HAHAHAHAHA-HAAA!

bleep bleep bleep

HELLO? OH, HI, MR. MANGELMANNER! YESSIR, WE-- ER, I TOOK CARE OF THE FLOOD!

YESSIR, I'M FINISHING THE CLEAN-UP RIGHT NOW! UHH, YOU WANT ME TO DO WHAT? WELL, YESSIR, IF YOU INSIST...

HEY, DID THE BOSS WANT YOU TO EVICT THAT "TRIBE OF LOST FOOD"?

NO, BUT HE ORDERED ME TO HOSE DOWN THE STORE'S ENTIRE PRODUCE SECTION! BUT NOW I'M SCARED THAT I MIGHT FLOOD THIS PLACE ALL OVER AGAIN!

END!

WATCH OUT FOR PAPERCUTZ™

Welcome to the spoilage-free second ANNOYING ORANGE. graphic novel from PAPERCUTZ. We're the folks dedicated to publishing great graphic novels for all ages. I'm your annoying Editor-in-Chief, Jim Salicrup, here to—

> HEY! HEY! JIM SAUERKRAUT!

Well, for Smurf's sake! Look who it is! That famously funny fruit and star of YouTube, Cartoon Network, and now Papercutz graphic novels-- ANNOYING ORANGE! Are you here to give us the inside poop on Dane Boedigheimer—

> WHAT DID YOU SAY? THERE'S POOP INSIDE YOUR OFFICE?! *THAT'S DISGUSTING!* MAYBE YOU SHOULD CALL YOURSELVES POOPERCUTZ? HAHAHAHAHA!

Oh, Orange! I can never get enough of your clever witticisms! Surely you know that "inside poop" is a quaint fun phrase for "inside information"! And as I was saying, you probably have some insights on Dane Boedigheimer—

> DANE BO-DING-DONG-HEIMER-WHAT?! THE ONLY DANEBO I KNOW IS THE SUPERMARKET I SPEND MOST OF MY TIME AT! MAYBE NERVILLE KNOWS WHO DANE BOE-DEE-OH-DOUGH IS, 'CAUSE I SURE DON'T! AND DON'T CALL ME "SHIRLEY."

Ha! There's that sophisticated wit of yours again! Well, even though you're pretending to be unaware of —

> NOW YOU'RE TALKING ABOUT HIS "UNDERWEAR"? WHAT KINDA COMPANY IS POOPERCUTZ? I THOUGHT YOU GUYS DID STUFF FOR ALL-AGES? I'M NOT SURE IF YOU GUYS SHOULD BE DOING MY GRAPHIC NOVELS AFTER ALL – YOU MAY BE TOO GRAPHIC!

You silly punster! You know full well that Mike Kazaleh and Scott Shaw! the writer/artists who create your comics are also contributors to your Cartoon Network show—

> WITH THOSE GUYS, YOU CAN START THE CARTOON NUTWORK! HAHAHAHA!

Be that as it may, we're almost out of room. I have just enough space left to tell everyone to keep an eye out for our next graphic novel, ANNOYING ORANGE #3 "Pulped Fiction"! Wow, I can't believe you let me finish that plug!

> HEY, I'M ANNOYING, *NOT STUPID!*

STAY IN TOUCH!

EMAIL: salicrup@papercutz.com
WEB: www.papercutz.com
TWITTER: @papercutzgn
FACEBOOK: PAPERCUTZGRAPHICNOVELS
REGULAR MAIL: Papercutz, 160 Broadway, Suite 700, East Wing, New York, NY 10038

DANE BOEDIGHEIMER

Dane (or Daneboe as he's known online) is a filmmaker and goofball extraordinaire. Dane spent most of his life in the glamorous Midwest, Harwood, North Dakota, to be exact. With nothing better to do, (it was North Dakota) at around the age of twelve, Dane began making short movies and videos with his parents' camcorder. Since then he has made hundreds, if not thousands of short web videos… many of which are only funny to him. But Dane has remained determined to make "the perfect short comedy film;" one that will end all social problems and bring laughter to all the children of the world.

Currently, Dane is most widely known for creating The Annoying Orange, one of the most successful web series ever. The Annoying Orange has over 2 million subscribers and over 1 billion video views on YouTube as well as over 11 million facebook fans. On top of that, The Annoying Orange has a top rated show on Cartoon Network! As a result, fans have clamored for all sorts of cool Annoying Orange toys, t-shirts, games, etc. And despite all the wonderful stuff

that has already appeared, fans still want more, and we suspect they'll be getting it.

Not to be completely undone, Dane's other videos have been viewed over 650 million times and have been featured on TV, as well as some of the most popular entertainment, news, and video sharing sites on the Internet.

In Dane's downtime he enjoys… oh, who are we kidding? Dane doesn't have any downtime. He wouldn't know what to do with himself if he did.

SPENCER GROVE

Spencer Grove has written plays, prose, television scripts and more online videos than any sane person should attempt. Also, he bakes a mean apple pie.

He began his career in independent productions, working on everything from infomercials to award shows, eventually moving to MTV where he served as an Associate Producer on Pimp My Ride. Since 2009, he has served as the head writer of the Annoying Orange web series, creating and co-creating the supporting cast and developing the ever-expanding online world of the Orange.

Below: A title card illustrated by Mike Kazaleh.

SCOTT SHAW!

Scott Shaw! is an example of Hunter S. Thompson's statement: "When the going gets weird, the weird turn pro." An award-winning cartoonist/writer of comicbooks, animation, advertising and toy design, Scott is also a historian of all forms of cartooning. After writing and drawing a number of underground "comix," Scott has worked on many mainstream comicbooks, including: SONIC THE HEDGEHOG (Archie); SIMPSONS COMICS, BART SIMPSON'S TREEHOUSE OF HORROR and RADIOACTIVE MAN (Bongo); WEIRD TALES OF THE RAMONES (Rhino); and his co-creation with Roy Thomas, CAPTAIN CARROT AND HIS AMAZING ZOO CREW! (DC). Scott has also worked on numerous animated cartoons, including: producing/directing of John Candy's Camp Candy (NBC/DIC/Saban) and Martin Short's The Completely Mental Misadventures of Ed Grimley (NBC/Hanna-Barbera Productions); Garfield and Friends (CBS/Film Roman); and the Emmy-winning Jim Henson's Muppet Babies (CBS/Marvel Productions).

Above: an example of Scott's storyboards for the ANNOYING ORANGE TV series

As Senior Art Director for the Ogilvy & Mather advertising agency, Scott worked on dozens of commercials for Post Pebbles cereals with the Flintstones. He also designed a line of Hanna-Barbera action figures for McFarlane Toys. Scott was one of the comic fans who organized the first San Diego Comic-Con, where he has become known for performing his hilarious ODDBALL COMICS slide show. shawcartoons.com. Scott is also a gag man and storyboard cartoonist on Cartoon Network's ANNOYING ORANGE program. His favorite fruit is forbidden.

MIKE KAZALEH

Mike Kazaleh is a veteran of comicbooks and animated cartoons. He began his career producing low budget commercials and sales films out of his tiny studio in Detroit, Michigan. Mike soon moved to Los Angeles, California and since then he has worked for most of the major cartoon studios and comicbook companies.

He has worked with such characters as The Flintstones, The Simpsons, Mighty Mouse, Krypto the Superdog, Ren and Stimpy, Cow and Chicken, and Bugs Bunny, as well as creating his own independent comics including THE ADVENTURES OF CAPTAIN JACK. Before all this stuff happened, Mike was a TV repairman.

Below: A title card designed by Mike Kazaleh.

FINALLY, DURIAN FRUIT IS SUBJECTED TO THE MOST GRUELING TEST OF THEM ALL!

OKAY, WE'RE GOING TO TURN IT UP TO A MAXIMUM OF *FOUR HUNDRED AND TWENTY POUNDS* PER SQUARE INCH!

POUND POUND POUND

BRING IT ON! I'M *TOUGH!* I CAN *TAKE* IT!

IS THAT *ALL* YOU'VE GOT? TURN UP THE PRESSURE. I'M NO *WIMP!* I COULD DO THIS ALL DAY!

WHY, I CAN--

KRAKKK

--I CAN'T BELIEVE M" NEARLY IMPENETRABL" SHELL JUST *CRACKE*

ARE YOU ALL RIGHT?

OH, I'LL BE OKAY... BUT THE INJURY HAS RELEASED PUTRESCENT *FUMES* FROM MY INTERIOR...

THIS IS *VULNAVIA TORIYAMA* AND I'M ON THE SCENE OF SON" SORT OF *CHEMICAL LEAK* OF SPILLAGE, WHICH IS ACCOMPANII" BY THE MOST AWFUL STENCH THAT THIS REPORTER HAS EVE" SMELLED! EVACUATIONS CONTINUE WHILE--

HEY, GUYS, LOOK! DURIAN FRUIT'S DOWNTOWN, MAKIN' A BIG OL' *STINK*-- AND HE'S GETTIN' PAID FOR" IT! HAHAHAHA-HAHA!

EN"

Withdrawn